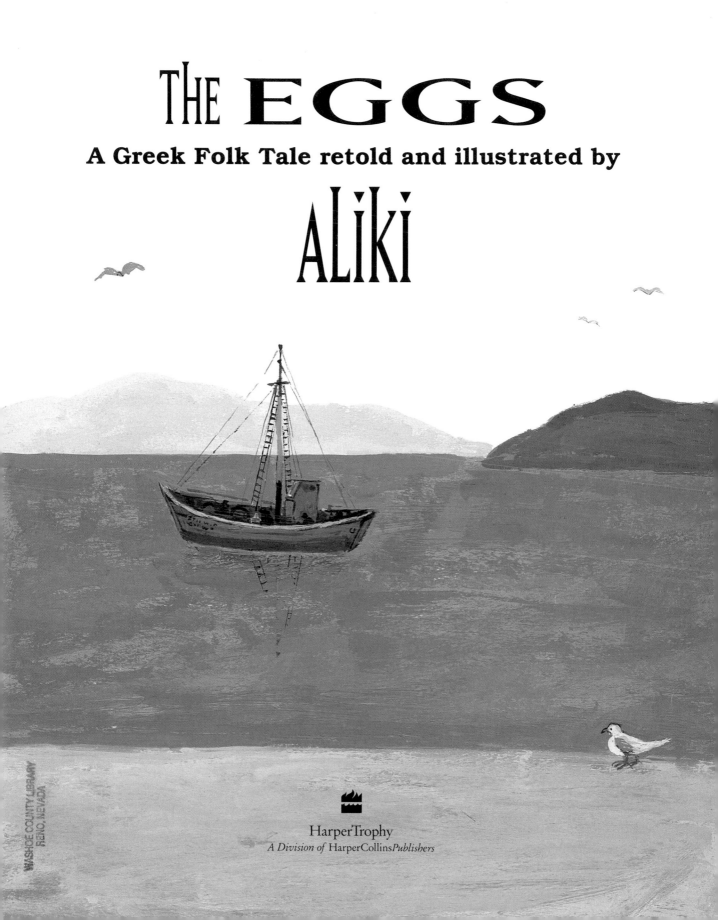

THE EGGS

A Greek Folk Tale retold and illustrated by

ALIKI

HarperTrophy
A Division of HarperCollins Publishers

Also by Aliki
Three Gold Pieces

For my grandmother
Stavroula Lagakos
on her ninety-first birthday

Once there was a sea captain whose most precious possession was his boat.

When he was not at sea, the captain scrubbed and patched and painted it.

His wife would shake her head and say,

"Heaven forbid that anything should happen to the caique."

The captain's life was not easy.

The sea was often dangerous, and the days away from his family were lonely. Yet, his happiest hours were those spent on his boat.

The captain knew all the ports well. He traveled to them with his cargo of fish or beans or olives.

It happened one day that he docked in a port he seldom visited.

As his crew unloaded the caique, the captain told them he was going to lunch.

He found an inn near the harbor and entered.

"Good afternoon," he said. "What do you have to eat?"

"Not a thing," answered the innkeeper. "We've run out of all the food. I just sent the boy to get some."

"Then I'll find another place to eat," said the hungry captain, and he turned to go.

"Wait!" said the innkeeper. "I was just frying four eggs in the kitchen. Maybe you'd like them."

"That's food to satisfy anybody's hunger," answered the captain, and he took a seat.

Just as he was finishing his meal, one of his sailors ran in.

"Quick, Captain!" he cried. "A storm is coming. We must leave at once."

The men ran out in such a hurry that the captain forgot to pay for the eggs.

Luckily, they sailed off before the winds could do the boat any damage.

Time passed. Back and forth the captain traveled, from
port to port.

At last, after six years, he returned to the place where he had eaten the eggs.

As soon as they docked, he went to the inn, for he had never forgotten his unpaid meal.

The captain greeted the innkeeper and explained who he was.

"Now I would like to pay for the eggs I ate six years ago," he said.

"Fine," said the innkeeper. "That will be five hundred gold pieces."

"What! Five hundred gold pieces!" cried the captain. "Who ever heard of such a price for four fried eggs?"

"My dear captain," said the sly innkeeper. "If I had those eggs, I would have put them under a hen. They would have hatched. I would have two hens and two cockerels. They would have grown and multiplied, and in six years I would have had a huge chicken farm. It could have brought me great wealth. I could just see myself now!

"Now, pay me or I'll take you to court."

The captain was in despair. Such a price would cost him his boat, his house and all his possessions. Besides, he would be in debt the rest of his life.

But the innkeeper would listen to no explanations.

"I will see you in court tomorrow," he shouted. "We will hear what the judge has to say."

The captain walked up and down the streets. The thought that he should lose his boat because of four eggs made his head spin.

He passed a taverna and decided to go in and think over his problem.

He found a seat in the crowded room and ordered a cup of coffee.

While he was sipping and brooding, he heard a voice ask,

"What's the matter my friend? You look distressed."

He glanced up and saw a friendly-looking man sitting nearby. It was he who had spoken.

In his misery, the captain told him his story.

"You have confided in the right person," the stranger said. "I am a lawyer. Now, buy me a glass of wine and I'll see that you don't lose your boat tomorrow."

The next morning the captain arrived in court at seven o'clock.

He saw the innkeeper in the crowded room, but nowhere could he find his lawyer.

He waited patiently.

One hour passed. Then another, and another.

At last everyone who had a case to be tried had finished and was gone.

By eleven o'clock the lawyer had still not arrived.

The judge grew impatient.

"I will wait until noon," he said. "After that there is nothing I can do."

Finally, at five minutes to twelve, the lawyer appeared.

"Good morning," he said pleasantly.

"And where have you been, sir?" asked the judge. "We have been here since seven o'clock and now we are nearly starved."

"I am sorry, Judge. But when you hear my story, you will know why I am so late," said the lawyer.

"Yesterday a friend gave me a sack of beans. My wife likes them so much, she cooked them. All of them. We ate beans for lunch. We ate beans for dinner. This morning we ate beans for breakfast. But we could not finish them. So we took the leftovers and planted them. Why, you should have seen us!"

"You planted the cooked beans?" laughed the innkeeper. "Who ever heard of cooked beans sprouting?"

The lawyer turned to him and said,

"AND WHO, SIR, EVER HEARD OF FRIED EGGS HATCHING?"

At once the innkeeper realized what he had done.

The judge ordered the captain to pay for his four eggs. The captain did it gladly. And to show his gratitude, he gave the innkeeper another handful of money.

"This is to fill my friend's glass full of wine whenever he gets thirsty," he said.

Then, happy and lighthearted, the captain went off
to his precious boat, and sailed home.